THIS BOOK BELONGS TO

Emily   Starks

_____

_____

REED

This beautiful story is for Natara Murray,
a very special person in my life.

POUNAMU'S STONES

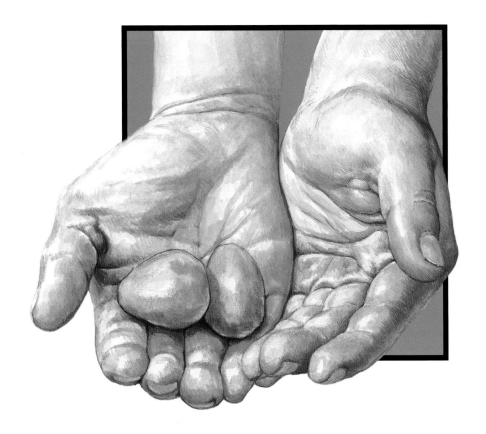

DOT MEHARRY
ILLUSTRATED BY BRUCE POTTER

REED

Many generations ago, a baby girl was born.
As was the tradition of the time, she was given to her grandmother,
who called her Pounamu, or treasured gift.

As she grew, Pounamu's grandmother taught her how to weave flax
to make kits. Pounamu also learned how to make flowers and birds by
weaving and twisting the flax in special ways.
Her young fingers were quick and nimble.

They used the flax kits they had made to gather shellfish. Best of all, Pounamu liked collecting pipi. She would tip the juice from the opened shells into her mouth and it would trickle down her chin. She would wipe her wet chin with the back of her hand and laugh.

Pounamu learned how to catch fish from the rocks and where to find the biggest mussels. She liked to wade into the rock pools and collect kina. She and her grandmother would open the kina and make loud, slurping noises as they sucked out the yellow eggs.

One day, Pounamu's grandmother showed her two stones.
Pounamu touched them. They were smooth and cold.

Her grandmother began to sing. As she sang she tapped the stones to the rhythm of her words. Pounamu began to sing too. Her body moved to the words of the song and the music of the stones.

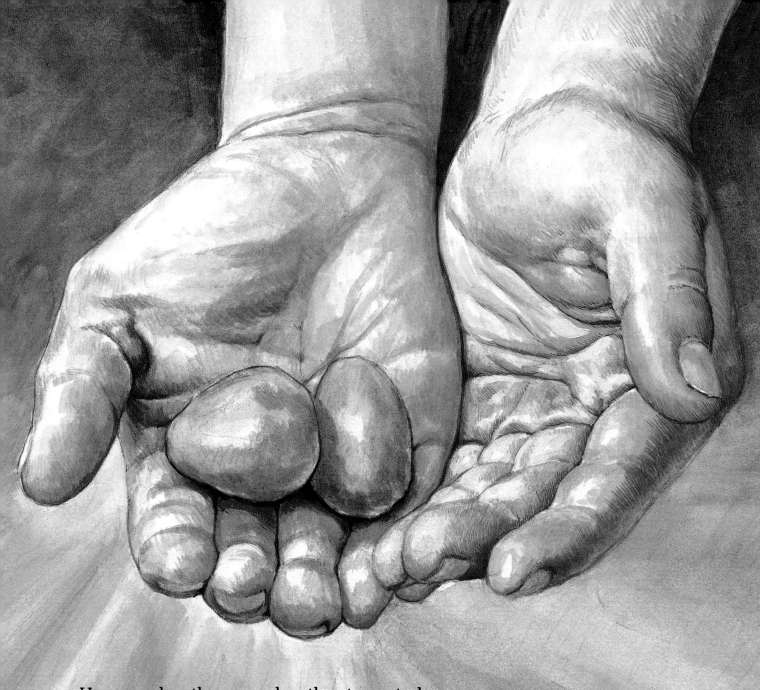

Her grandmother gave her the stones to keep.
'These are special stones,' she said. 'They are like you, Pounamu, a treasured gift.'

Pounamu made a small flax bag for her stones and tied it around her neck. She would keep them close to her heart.

As the years passed Pounamu's grandmother told her many stories of their ancestors. Mostly Pounamu loved the stories of her grandmother when she was a young girl. Pounamu learned how, in days long gone, her grandmother called dolphins with the stones in the flax bag.

Pounamu would clasp the small flax bag in her hand and dream of her grandmother standing at the water's edge with her stones. Her heart would beat faster and faster, as though there were something inside of her that knew more than she understood.

One summer Pounamu's grandmother called her family back home. They came from all over the land. They collected shellfish and caught fish from the rocks. They sucked the yellow eggs from the kina.

They listened as Pounamu spoke about her life with her grandmother. Pounamu told them stories of their ancestors that her grandmother had told her. They sang and laughed and sang some more. It was a time of togetherness.

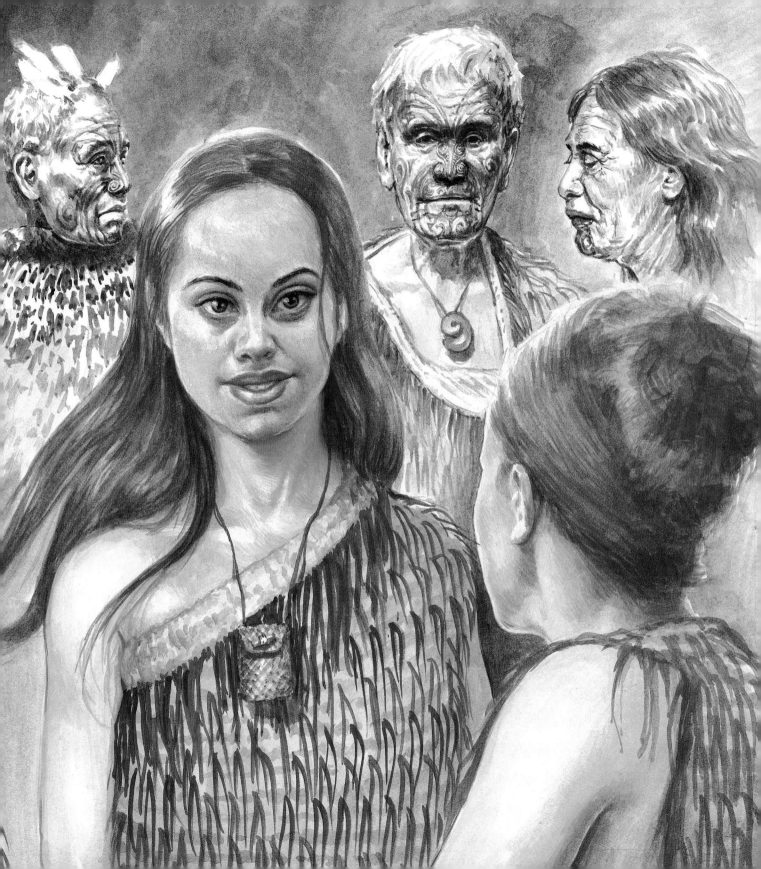

After they had gone, Pounamu walked down to the rocks. She missed the family. She wondered why she was the one who had been chosen for her grandmother. She took her stones out of the flax bag around her neck and held one in the palm of her hand, tapping it with the other as she opened and closed her fingers. The stones warmed against her skin as she played.

As darkness closed in, the night air wrapped itself around her body like a cloak. Suddenly her heart began to beat faster and faster, just as it did when her grandmother had talked of calling the dolphins.

Pounamu began to sing softly as a sea breeze marked the changing tide.
The sound of the stones and Pounamu's voice rose and fell, like the waves
rolling to the shore. She held the stones in her closed hands and waited.

At first there was nothing. Then she heard them as they swam
nearer and nearer.
'The dolphins,' she whispered.

It was late when she returned to the house.
'They came,' shouted Pounamu. 'They came!'
Pounamu knelt by her grandmother and took hold of her frail hands.
Tears flowed down her grandmother's old and wrinkled face.

'You were a gift to me, my Pounamu,' whispered her grandmother.
'And they are my gift to you.'

ABOUT THE AUTHOR

Dot Meharry was born in Taumarunui and spent her school years on the family sheep farm. After spending some time teaching in the country, she taught in London, before returning to New Zealand to marry and raise a family. She lives with her husband, Jack, in Thames, on the Coromandel Peninsula, where she has taught for many years.

Dot has written books which are used to teach reading in New Zealand, Australia and America, and she finds this particularly satisfying.

These days Dot and Jack job share a teaching role, which allows Dot time to write, relax at the beach and to spend time with their grandchildren.

Other books by Dot Meharry
Dance for Me
Paint What You See
The Pipi and the Mussels – Nga Kutai Me Nga Pipi

ABOUT THE ILLUSTRATOR

Bruce Potter began his art career as a cartoonist and caricaturist for a number of different newspapers around the world. He has been self-employed as a portrait painter specialising in oils, and he started illustrating children's books about four years ago. Bruce lives on two acres of land in Tuakau, south of Auckland, with his wife and three children, all of whom have appeared in his books at one time or another.

To date Bruce has illustrated the following books for Reed:
Matariki, The Treasure and *Child of Aoteroa* by Melanie Drewery,
and *The Donkey Man* by Glyn Harper.

Reed Publishing (NZ) Ltd
Te Karuhi tā tāpui o Reed (Aotearoa)

Established in 1907, Reed is New Zealand's largest
book publisher, with over 300 titles in print.

For details on all these books visit our website:
www.reed.co.nz

Published by Reed Children's Books, a division of Reed Publishing (NZ) Ltd,
39 Rawene Road, Birkenhead, Auckland 10. Associated companies, branches
and representatives throughout the world.

© 2004 Dot Meharry — text
© 2004 Bruce Potter — illustrations
The author and illustrator assert their moral rights in the work.

National Library of New Zealand Cataloguing-in-Publication Data
Meharry, Dot.
Pounamu's stones / Dot Meharry ; illustrated by Bruce Potter.
ISBN 1-86948-512-2
[1. Grandmothers—Fiction. 2. Grandparent and child—Fiction.
3. Maori (New Zealand people)—Fiction.] I. Potter, Bruce (Bruce
Anthony). II. Title.
NZ823.2—dc 22

ISBN 1 86948 512 2
First published 2004

Edited by Carolyn Lagahetau
Designed by Cheryl Rowe

Printed in China